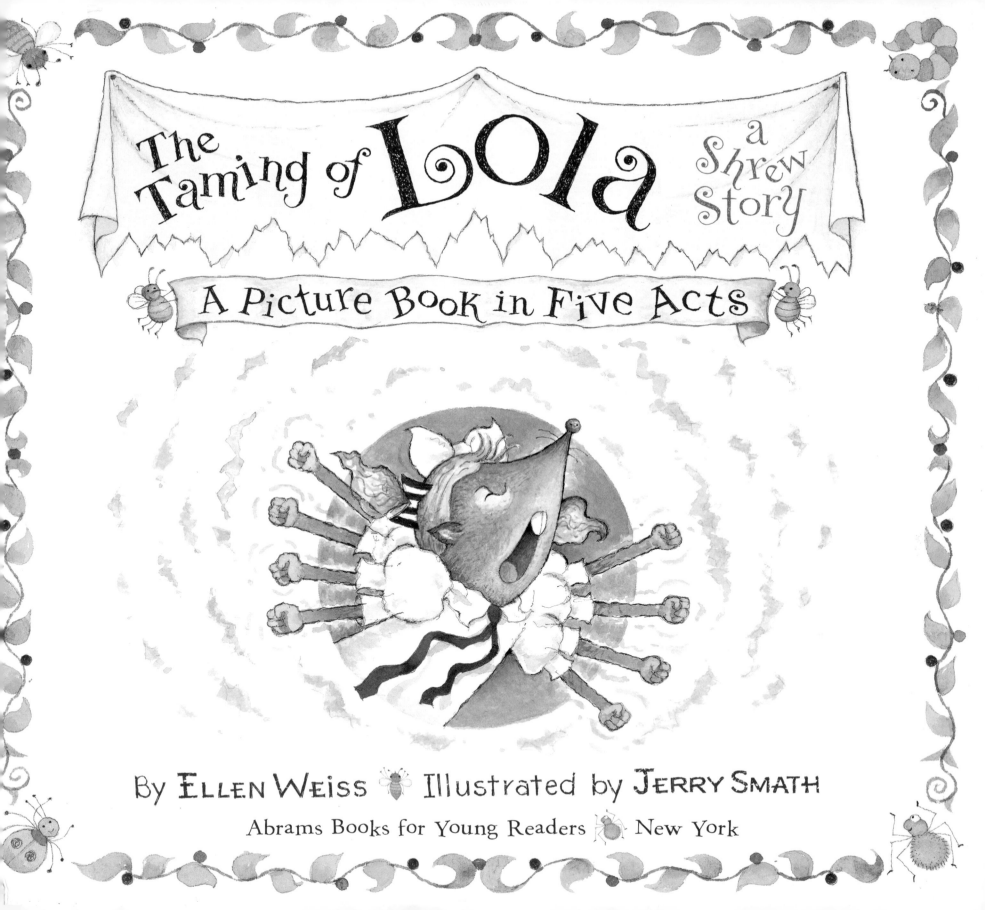

The Taming of Lola
a Shrew Story

A Picture Book in Five Acts

By ELLEN WEISS · Illustrated by JERRY SMATH

Abrams Books for Young Readers · New York

For Mel
—E. W.

To my grandson: Jonathan Andrew Smath
—J. S.

The art in this book was done in watercolor on Fabriano Artistico
soft watercolor paper with pen-and-ink accents.

Library of Congress Cataloging-in-Publication Data

Weiss, Ellen, 1949–
The taming of Lola: A shrew story/ by Ellen Weiss ; illustrated by Jerry Smath.
p. cm.
Summary: Lola, a shrew, is famous all over the West Meadow for her temper tantrums, but when her cousin Lester comes for a visit and gets
special treatment just because he demands it, Lola begins to rethink her behavior.
ISBN 978-0-8109-4066-6
[1. Temper tantrums—Fiction. 2. Behavior—Fiction. 3. Cousins—Fiction. 4. Shrews—Fiction. 5. Grandmothers—Fiction.] I. Smath, Jerry,
ill. II. Title.

PZ7.W4472Tam 2010
[E]—dc22
2009000617

Printed and bound in China
10 9 8 7 6 5 4 3 2

Abrams Books for Young Readers are available at special discounts when purchased in quantity for premiums and promotions as well as
fundraising or educational use. Special editions can also be created to specification. For details, contact specialmarkets@abramsbooks.com or the
address below.

THE ART OF BOOKS SINCE 1949
115 West 18th Street
New York, NY 10011
www.abramsbooks.com

Lola was a shrew. She lived with her family in a burrow under a big spruce tree, at the edge of the West Meadow. They led a very busy life, eating bugs and worms and whatnot all day long.

Although she was very, very tiny, Lola had a big temper. Shrews are not known for being nice, but Lola really took the cake.

She was so stubborn and bad-tempered that all her brothers and sisters stayed away from her as often as possible.

If Lola was given mayflies for breakfast when she wanted slugs, she had conniptions.

If she was asked to wear her red socks when she wanted to wear her blue ones, she threw herself on the floor and had a tantrum.

She was famous all over the West Meadow for her temper.

Lola had such an awful temper that, after a while, everyone began to let her have her way.

"I don't want to take a bath!" she would scream.

"All right, dear," her mother would say.

"I will *not* eat yesterday's mosquitoes!" she would yell. "I would rather eat *mud* than yesterday's mosquitoes!"

"Okay," her father would say with a sigh. "We'll catch some fresh ones."

Act II

One day, Lola's mother made an announcement at dinner. "Guess who's coming to stay with us for awhile?"

"I don't want anyone to come stay with us," said Lola. "Who is it?"

"It's your cousin Lester, from the East Meadow. He's just your age. I know you'll have a wonderful time with him."

When they tell you you're going to have a wonderful time with somebody, **WATCH OUT**!

Lola had four hundred and twenty-three cousins. Lester was not
one she had met. She didn't want to meet him, either.

"He can come," said Lola darkly, "but if he thinks I'm going to
share my stuff with him, he's got another think coming."

The next morning, Lester appeared at the door. Lola hated him immediately.

"Come in, dear," Lola's mother said to Lester. "We have some nice spider pie all made."

"I hate spider pie," said Lester. "I won't eat it."

"Won't you just give it a little taste?"

"NO!" roared Lester.

"Okay, okay," said Lola's mother. "You can have anything you want for breakfast."

"That's better," said Lester. "I want grubs. Fried grubs."

Lola was so shocked, she was unable to speak.

"And I want them *now*!" added Lester.

Lola had heard enough. Her voice returned, loud and clear.

"Hey, wait just a minute, buster!" she yelled. "You don't get to act like that! This is my house, and only *I* get to act like that!"

"Says who?" Lester retorted.

"Says me!" yelled Lola.

"Who cares?"

"I care!" said Lola, stamping her foot.

Lester stamped even harder. "Well, I don't care if you care!" he said.

Neither one of them noticed that Lola's mother had backed away.

Lola screamed.

Lester screamed back.

After half an hour, their voices were beginning to give out.
But neither one of them had given in.

Act III

When it was bedtime, Lola's father took Lester through the twisty tunnels to the sleeping quarters. "Here's Lola's bed," he said, "and here's yours, Lester."

"I don't like this one," said Lester. "I want *hers*."

"But, Lester, that's Lola's bed."

"I DON'T CARE! I WANT THAT ONE!"

"All right, Lester. I guess Lola can get used to the other one," Lola's father said with a sigh.

BEDTIME FOR SHREWS

LOLA

"What's going on?" Lola cried. "How come he gets anything he wants just because he yells and screams?"

Lola's father just shrugged. "It works pretty well for you," he said.

"I don't like you," said Lola to Lester.

"The feeling is mutual," said Lester.

"You can't sleep in my bed," said Lola.

"Yes, I can," said Lester.

Well, Lola and Lester kept yelling for three hours, until they were hoarse.

Finally, they lay on the floor, all tantrumed out.

The moon came up.

The floor was hard.

"Are you ready to give in?" whispered Lola.

"No," Lester croaked.

When Lola's mother and father came upstairs the next morning, they found both of them still on the floor, sound asleep.

Act IV

But the war was not over. It started right up again after breakfast.

"I want to make a tunnel," said Lester.

"Well, I want to go swimming," said Lola. "And I'm in charge."

"Says who?" said Lester.

"Says me!" Lola replied.

"You are a great big foo-face!" said Lester.

"Oh, yeah? Well, you are . . . a great big *huge* foo-face!" Lola retorted.

And once again, they were off.

"Well, you are the biggest foo-face in the entire world!" yelled Lester.

"You are bigger than the biggest foo-face that ever lived!" yelled Lola.

They yelled at each other all morning, not even noticing when Lola's whole family left to go on a picnic.

They yelled all afternoon.

As it grew darker, Lola noticed that she was hungry. Then she realized that she had not eaten since breakfast. She had been too busy arguing with Lester.

Lester kept yelling, but Lola grew quiet. She was thinking. Lester yelled and yelled, and Lola thought and thought.

She waited for Lester to finish what he was yelling.
". . . And furthermore," he was shouting, "you don't know one single thing about fried grubs!"

Here comes the brilliant speech. **READY?**

Lola looked at him. "Lester," she said, "I've been thinking."

"Yeah, well—" said Lester, getting ready to say something mean.

"Shh," said Lola. "I've been thinking. We have been fighting with each other every second since you got here. We did not get to sleep in our beds last night. We did not go swimming *or* make tunnels *or* go on a picnic today. And our throats are very sore."

"So?" said Lester.

"So," said Lola, "I think we need to work something out."

"I guess *I am* sort of hungry," Lester admitted.

Act V

And so, Lester and Lola worked something out.

They did not exactly become friends. But they did manage to get along, more or less. They took turns . . . a little. They shared . . . a little. Lola even let Lester sleep in her bed now and then, especially when it had a lot of crumbs in it. And once Lester lent Lola his red hat, though it did have a sort of funny smell.

At last the day came for Lester to return home. Lola watched him pack up his little suitcases. "Good-bye, Mr. Giant Foo-Face," she said.

"Good-bye, Mrs. Giant Foo-Face," he replied.

"I'm not sad to see you go," Lola said.

"I'm not sad to leave," he said.

After Lester was gone, things were very quiet in Lola's house.
At dinnertime, Lola let her little sister eat the biggest mosquitoes.
Somehow, it just didn't seem quite as important to have a tantrum about it.

That night, Lola lay in her bed. The bed Lester had slept in was empty.

Then a tiny voice came wafting over the fields from the East Meadow.

"Good night, Mrs. Foo-Face!" it called.

"Good night, Mr. Foo-Face!"

Lola called back.

Then she smiled and went to sleep.